ON PURPOSE

Written by Stacie Thomas

Illustrated by Jeremiah Gould

"I will praise thee; for I am fearfully and wonderfully made; marvelous are thy works; and that my soul knoweth right well."

PSALM 139:14

First published in 2024 by Enjoying the Journey in partnership with Faithworks Media. Enjoying the Journey exists to evangelize the lost with the gospel of Jesus Christ, encourage pastors and local churches, and equip believers to walk with God and serve Him each day. Through audio, video, and print resources we are seeking to preach the gospel, teach the Word of God, and reach this generation for Christ.

Faithworks Media provides high-quality church print resources and evangelistic material which *"adorn the doctrine of God our Saviour in all things."*

Editing, proofreading, and assistance by Tammy Jones, Brittani Shackleford, and Becky Dowdy.

ISBN 978-1-958301-02-9
Printed in the United States of America

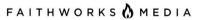

"For the Furtherance of the Gospel" » **faithworks**media.com

Acknowledgements

To my loving husband Ty: thank you for encouraging me to write this book when it was still just a dream in my heart. Thank you for helping and supporting me through the entire process. I could never have done it without you. You are my best friend, and I love you with all my heart.

To my children, Micah, Caden and Sydney: I love being your mom! You are a gift from God, and the inspiration for this book. May you always remember that you were made by God for a purpose.

To my one and only brother Scott: thank you for giving of your time to answer ALL my questions , and for your advice and guidance in the publishing of this book. I am thankful to have you as my brother, and my friend. It is true what they say, "That's what big brothers are for!"

To my parents: thank you for instilling in me at an early age that every life is precious to God. Thank you for encouraging me to be exactly who God made me to be - nothing more and nothing less. You are my heroes. I love you both!

A Note To Parents, Teachers And Children's Workers:

Our children are growing up in a society that is full of confusion and uncertainty. There are countless young people that do not have any idea who they are, or where they came from. They feel alone and without hope. As followers of Christ, we have the answer- Jesus Christ! They need to know the life-changing truths found in the Word of God. It is our responsibility to proclaim the truth to the next generation. Psalm 145:4 says, "One generation shall praise thy works to another, and shall declare thy mighty acts." This book, in all its simplicity, was written for that exact purpose. It is designed to teach children of all ages that God created them, loves them, and has a plan for their life. There are Scripture verses written out in the back of this book that correspond with each page in the book. Here are a few tips on how to read this book with children:

1 As you read each page, be sure to read the corresponding Scripture as well. It is important that children understand that these verses were given to us by God! Remember that a child may not understand every word, so be prepared to explain the verses as you go.

2 Take your time and encourage questions – this is how children learn!

3 Use this book as a Scripture memory tool for children. It is crucial that children begin hiding God's Word in their heart at an early age.

4 Take them to the Gospel page at the end of the book and show them from the Word of God how they can trust Jesus as their personal Savior. It is the most important decision they will ever make.

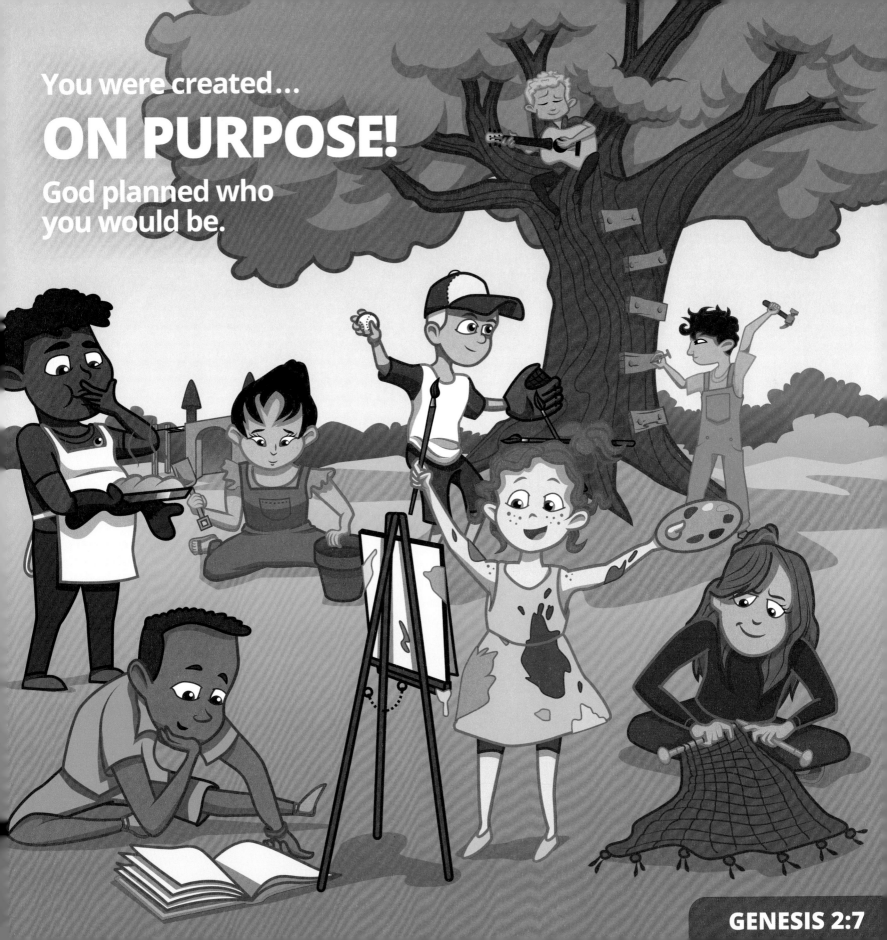

He made you a **BOY,** or He made you a **GIRL.**
He chose your personality.

GENESIS 1:27

You may be tall, you may be short.

Your eyes may be **BROWN, GREEN,** or **BLUE.**

However God made you,
He made you **JUST RIGHT!**
When He formed you,
He knew just what to do.

JEREMIAH 1:5A, PSALM 139:13

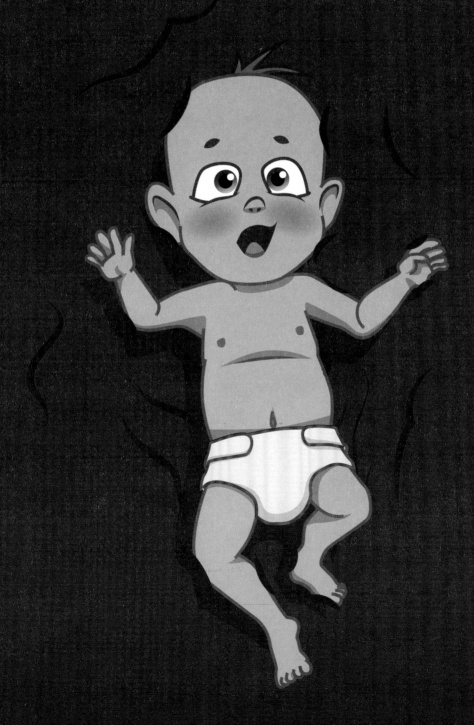

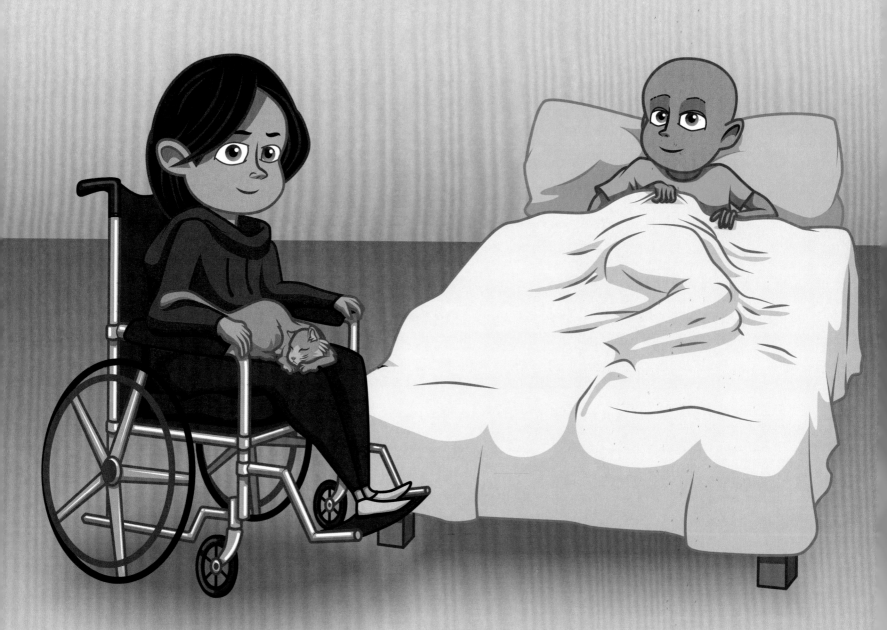

You are not a **MISTAKE,** mix up, or blunder.
There is something **important**
God has for **YOU** to do!

PSALM 18:30

Read **GOD'S WORD**
And you will find —
You did not come from a chimpanzee!

You are loved...On purpose!
God **SENT HIS SON** to die **FOR ALL MEN**
He is the **only** way to Heaven.

I JOHN 4:10

He loves you even when you do wrong,
And He knows the number of **hairs on your head!**

MATTHEW 10:29-31

He paid the price for your sin
When He died on the **CROSS** of Calvary.

JOHN 3:16

So why were you created?
To bring **GLORY TO GOD.**
And God **never** makes a mistake.

Thank Him today for making you —YOU!

You are **fearfully** and **wonderfully** made!

BIBLE VERSES

(p. 3) Genesis 2:7
And the Lord God formed man of the dust of the ground, and breathed into his nostrils the breath of life; and man became a living soul.

(p. 4) Genesis 1:27
So God created man in his own image, in the image of God created he him; male and female created he them.

(p. 5) Psalm 139:17
How precious also are thy thoughts unto me O God! How great is the sum of them!

(p. 6) Jeremiah 1:5a
Before I formed thee in the belly I knew thee. . .

Psalm 139:13
For thou hast possessed my reins; thou hast covered me in my mother's womb.

(p. 7) Isaiah 43:7
Even every one that is called by my name; for I have created him for my glory, I have formed him; yea, I have made him.

(p. 8) Psalm 18:30
As for God his way is perfect: the word of the Lord is tried: he is a buckler to all those that trust in him.

(p. 9) Ephesians 2:10
For we are his workmanship, created in Christ Jesus unto good works, which God hath before ordained that we should walk in them.

(p. 10) Genesis 1:26
And God said, Let us make man in our image, after our likeness; and let them have dominion over the fish of the sea, and over the fowl of the air, and over the cattle and over all the earth, and over every living thing that moveth upon the earth.

(p. 11) I John 4:10
Herein is love; not that we loved God, but that He loved us and sent His son to be the propitiation for our sins.

(p. 12) Romans 10:13
For whosoever shall call upon the name of the Lord shall be saved.

(p. 13) I Peter 5:7
Casting all your care upon Him for He careth for you.

(p. 14) Matthew 10:29-31
Are not two sparrows sold for a farthing? And one of them shall not fall on the ground without your Father. But the very hairs of our head are all numbered . Fear ye not therefore, ye are of more value than many sparrows.

(p. 15) I John 3:1-2
Behold what manner of love the Father hath bestowed upon us, that we should be called the sons of God. . .

(p. 16) John 3:16
For God so loved the world that he gave his only begotten Son that whosoever believeth in him should not perish but have everlasting life.

(p. 17) Revelation 4:11
Thou art worthy O Lord to receive glory and honour and power; for thou hast created all things, and for thy pleasure they are and were created.

(p. 18) Psalm 139:14
I will praise thee; for I am fearfully and wonderfully made; marvelous are thy works; and that my soul knoweth right well.

THE GOSPEL

God created us, knows us, and loves us. God wants us to know Him too! Let me show you how....

ADMIT THAT YOU ARE A SINNER.

Romans 3:23 says, "For all have sinned and come short of the glory of God." We are all sinners. Because of our sin we deserve death.

BELIEVE THAT GOD SENT HIS SON, JESUS, TO DIE FOR YOUR SINS.

John 3:16 says, "For God so loved the world that he gave his only begotten Son, that whosoever believeth in him should not perish but have everlasting life."

1

Jesus died on the cross.

2

He was buried in a tomb.

3

In 3 days he rose again.

I Corinthians 15:3-4 "For I delivered unto you first of all that which I also received, how that Christ died for our sins according to the scriptures. And that he was buried, and that he rose again the third day according to the scriptures."

THIS IS THE GOSPEL!

CALL UPON THE LORD JESUS TO FORGIVE YOUR SIN AND SAVE YOU. HE IS THE ONLY WAY TO HEAVEN.

Romans 10:13 says, "For whosoever shall call upon the name of the Lord shall be saved."

Meet The Author

Stacie Thomas has served alongside her husband Ty for many years in church ministry and Christian education. They have been blessed with three children: Micah, Caden, and Sydney, and make their home in the mountains of West Virginia. Stacie is a dedicated wife and mother, long time school teacher, and lifelong student of Scripture. She is committed to helping the next generation come to know God through His Word.

For additional resources for your family and Christian living visit **EnjoyingtheJourney.org.**

Following God's Word · **Finding** Christ's Joy

Thank you for your prayers and support.